The Snatchabook

STORY BY
HELEN DOCHERTY

ILLUSTRATED BY
THOMAS DOCHERTY

One dark, dark night in Burrow Down,
A rabbit called Eliza Brown
Found a book and settled down . . .

When a Snatchabook
flew into town.

In every house,
in every bed,
A bedtime book
was being read.

Tales of dragons, spitting flames;

Witches playing spooky games;

Pirates on the seven seas;

Princesses, trying to sleep on peas.

And every child, in every bed,
Listened hard to each word said.

Eliza Brown, at Number Three,
Was reading quite contentedly.

Her curtains opened, just a chink.
She barely had a chance to blink.
Her story book just disappeared!

Eliza found that very weird.

The little owls, on Mummy's lap,
Were quite surprised to hear a tap
Against their bedroom window pane.
Tap, tap! They heard the noise again.
Before they'd even looked around,
The book was gone – without a sound.

The wind blew wild across the sky.
The smallest squirrel heard a cry.
"What's that?" she whispered to her Dad.

But then – *and this was really bad* –
Before they'd had a chance to look,
She'd lost her very favourite book.

And so it went, night after night.
Books disappeared from left and right.
Five books here and six books there –
The shelves began to look quite bare.

In Burrow Down the rumours spread
Of book thieves under every bed.
Eliza Brown, at Number Three,
Was keen to solve the mystery.

She planned one night to lie in wait
And use a pile of books as bait.

Long hours passed without a peep
(She'd nearly fallen fast asleep)

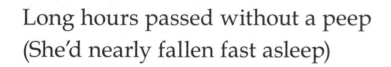

When, suddenly, Eliza heard
A flap of wings:
a bat?
A bird?

Eliza saw a shadow loom,
Enormous – right across her room.
What kind of monster could it be?
Eliza thought: "You don't scare me!"

And yet, her heart was beating fast –
She'd have to face the thief at last . . .

She threw the window open wide
And shouted to the Thing outside:
"Stop stealing
all our books,
right now!
Just give them back,
I don't care how!"

"I'm sorry," came a little voice.
"I really am. I had no choice."
Eliza looked down in surprise;
She couldn't quite believe her eyes.
"So who are YOU? And what's your name?"

The creature hung its head in shame.
He mumbled, with a mournful look,
"I'm just a little Snatchabook."

Eliza nodded solemnly.
She sat the creature on her knee.
"You can't just come and help yourself
To every book on every shelf!"

A tear rolled from the creature's eye,
And softly he began to cry:
"I know it's wrong, but can't you see –
I've got no one to read to me!"

Eliza sighed. He looked so sad.
If he just had a mum or dad
To read him stories every night –
Well, then he might behave all right!

That very night,
they hatched a plan:

And so, the Snatchabook began . . .

. . . To give back all the books he'd nicked.

(Eliza Brown was very strict.)

And, trying hard to prove himself,

He stacked them neatly

on each shelf.

And when he'd made his full amends,
Eliza called on all her friends,
And told them how he'd worked all night
To turn a wrong into a right.

And now each night in Burrow Down,
As darkness falls upon the town,
In every house, in every bed,
A bedtime book is being read.

And if you take a closer look
You might just see the Snatchabook,
Perched happily on someone's bed . . .
Listening hard to each word said.

For our parents, who always read to us,
and for our daughters, Lucia and Bethan.

First published in 2013 by Alison Green Books
An imprint of Scholastic Children's Books
Euston House, 24 Eversholt Street
London NW1 1DB
A division of Scholastic Ltd
www.scholastic.co.uk
London – New York – Toronto – Sydney – Auckland
Mexico City – New Delhi – Hong Kong

Text copyright © 2013 Helen Docherty
Illustrations copyright © 2013 Thomas Docherty

HB ISBN: 978 1 407116 53 2
PB ISBN: 978 1 407116 54 9